SILAS

WOLVES OF THE RISING SUN #5

KENZIE COX

Published by Bayou Moon Press, LLC, 2015.

This is a work of fiction. Similarities to real people, places, or events are entirely coincidental.

Silas: WOLVES OF THE RISING SUN #5
First edition.

Copyright © 2015 Kenzie Cox.
Written by Kenzie Cox.

Join the Packs of the Mating Season

The mating moon is rising…

Wherever that silver light touches, lone male werewolves are seized by the urge to find their mates. Join these six packs of growly alpha males (with six-packs!) as they seek out the smart, sassy women who are strong enough to claim them forever.

The "Mating Season" werewolf shifter novellas are brought to you by six authors following the adventures of six different packs. Each novella is the story of a mated pair (or trio!) with their Happily Ever After. Enjoy the run!

Learn more at thematingseason.com

SILAS: WOLVES OF THE RISING SUN

He's not supposed to love her…

Silas Davenne has wanted Hannah Valentine since the day he walked into her life six years ago. The problem? He promised her mother he'd protect her from his dangerous shifter life. And Silas Davenne never breaks a promise.

Hannah Valentine is on a mission. She wants Silas Davenne. After years of sexual tension brewing between them, she's determined to either become his mate or move on for good. But after one tragic night, suddenly fate has other plans.

Sign up for Kenzie's newsletter here at www.kenziecox.com. Do you prefer text messages? Sign up for text alerts! Just text SHIFTERSROCK to 24587 to register.

CHAPTER 1

HANNAH

If there was one thing I knew how to do, it was catch the eye of Silas Davenne. The former Marine stood shirtless in the kitchen of the high-end cabin he was building, piercing me with his intense gaze. The type that said he wanted to devour me in every way possible.

On any other day, I'd have stared right back, willing him to do just that. To finally make good on the silent promise he'd been torturing me with for six long years. Six freakin' years of him undressing me with his eyes and watching my every move without doing a damned thing about it. Except that one time. The one burned into my brain that had made everything a million times worse.

But today was different. Today I was pissed as hell.

"You're a real piece of work, you know that?" I said, for once not moved by his broad shoulders, narrow waist, or perfectly sculpted abs.

He frowned and furrowed his brow in confusion. "What are you talking about?"

"Does this look familiar?" I brandished a crumpled-up note. One with a phone number and the name Colin Graham scrawled across it.

He stiffened and averted his eyes for just a moment.

His reaction told me everything I needed to

know. He was guilty as sin. A fresh surge of righteous anger shot through me but was immediately tempered by gratification at the knowledge he had tried to keep me from dating someone else. I shook my head, frustrated with my reaction. He did not get to control my love life.

Especially since he'd made it perfectly clear he wasn't interested in being a part of it.

Liar, the voice in the back of my head whispered. The crumpled-up message was just one more thing in a long list of reasons why I didn't believe him.

"That guy is trouble, Hannah." He turned his back on me and picked up a cabinet door.

"What?" My voice was cold, hard as steel.

He didn't even flinch as he secured the door to the hinge. Damn him for being a badass former military man. Nothing fazed him. Maybe if I unzipped my sundress and showed him exactly what I wasn't wearing underneath.

I was certain that would make things go from zero to ninety in less than half a second. But I'd be damned if I let him have me after the shit he'd just pulled.

"Silas," I said, trying to soften my tone. I'd learned a long time ago anger didn't work on him. Not from me. It was when my words were gentle and seemed to touch something in him that I could finally get through.

"Give me a minute," he said, not missing a beat as he focused all his attention on installing the cabinet door, making sure it was perfectly aligned. Silas and the rest of the Davenne brothers owned the Bayou Hidden Resort, and Silas took great pride in the luxury cabins he designed and built. Normally I admired his dedication, but today I wanted to smack the tools out of his hands and force him to give me his undivided attention. To put my feelings first for once.

When he turned around, I was leaning against the breakfast bar with my arms crossed over my chest, silently seething.

He raised an eyebrow, indicating it was time for me to talk.

I wanted to scream.

But I swallowed it and said, "It is not your job to protect me—"

"The hell it isn't. You know I promised Lydia I'd take care of you."

That again? I knew how much my mother had meant to him. She'd been the one stable mother figure in his life, and he'd have moved heaven and earth to do anything she wanted. But this was going too far. "Promising my mother you'd take care of me does not mean locking me away in an office and keeping me from having a life."

"Your mom—"

"Stop it. Mom wouldn't have wanted me to be sitting home on Saturday nights while everyone else is out having fun. Dating. Finding mates."

His expression immediately shut down, and in a flat tone he said, "Not everyone is looking for mates."

"Oh, believe me, I got that message loud and clear." The attempt to keep my anger buried had failed miserably. "But you can't have it both ways, Silas. Just because you think we shouldn't be together doesn't give you the right to run my life."

"That's not… Shit." He scowled. "That's not why I got rid of the note."

"No? Then please. Do tell." I waved a hand. "What's wrong with him? Too smart? Too tall? Too handsome?"

His eyes narrowed in irritation. "Don't be insulting, Hannah."

I threw my hands up, my patience completely gone. "Only if you stop being so patronizing."

We stared each other down for a long moment. Then finally Silas's features hardened and he said, "It's his family. His uncle, who raised him, was incarcerated for corruption, and he has ties to the Hunters. It's highly likely this guy is only trying to get to you because of us."

"You don't know that," I said, but doubt

crept in. Why would he say that if it wasn't true?

"I do know. I checked."

"You did a background check on a guy who called to ask me out on a date?" I asked, incredulous.

He nodded without hesitation, completely confident in his actions.

"Geez, Silas," I said, shaking my head in exasperation as my anger dissipated. The Hunters were a hate group that went after the shifter community. If I'd known Colin was in any way affiliated with a known threat, I'd never have given him my number in the first place. But even so, running background checks on anyone who phoned me was way over the line. "You can't just go around digging up dirt on every person who tries to talk to me."

"I'll do what I have to," he said with finality, as if the conversation was over.

I stalked up to him, my eyes narrowed and my teeth clenched. "You listen to me, Silas Davenne. I am not yours to save. And just because you found something on Colin that *might* make him dangerous, that does not make it okay for you to interfere with who my friends are."

His expression was blank, but then everything about him softened as he brushed a lock of hair behind my ear. "Yes, Hann. You *are* mine."

CHAPTER 2
SILAS

Hannah sucked in a sharp breath and took a step back. "Don't say that."

"Why? It's what you want to hear, isn't it?" I was being a dick and I knew it. Saying she was mine without having any intention of claiming her was fucked up. But dammit, she'd given that douchebag the main number to the resort that I, along with my two brothers, owned. Since I was here day in and day out, she had to know there was a strong possibility I'd be the one answering the phone.

"No." Her gaze swept down my chest for just a moment before she jerked her head. The faint scent of her arousal permeated my senses, and it was all I could do to not press her up against the wall right there and take her as mine, once and for all.

Off-limits. Wren's voice rang in my head, making me take my own step back.

And that was the crux of the problem right there. Wren was her half brother. They shared a mother. But Wren was my half brother as well, and we shared a father. So while Hannah and I weren't technically related in any way, the rest of the world assumed we were stepsiblings. We weren't. We hadn't even grown up together. In fact, I hadn't met her until two days before her eighteenth birthday.

I'd been fresh off the plane from the Middle

East, discharge papers in hand, when I'd gotten the phone call from Wren. His mother was sick and since he'd been deployed, he needed me to take care of her and Hannah. He hadn't even had to ask. I had fond memories of Lydia when she'd dated our father, before Hannah was born. She'd been the only adult to ever give a shit about any of us. I'd spent nine months getting Lydia to and from her doctor's appointments and helping her get her affairs in order. In the end, all she'd wanted from me was to watch over Hannah.

Only Hannah hadn't needed anyone to take care of her. She hadn't then and sure as hell didn't now. But that wasn't going to stop me. I'd made a promise, and I intended to keep it.

"Listen," I said to Hannah, squaring my shoulders. "Since you're human and you've insisted upon living with a pack of wolves, that means you *are* mine. As far as the rest of the world is concerned, you do belong to me. To us. Darien and Wren and myself. Why do you think no one ever bothers you?"

"Because you're a bully?" She raised both of her eyebrows in challenge.

I shook my head, more amused than irritated. "Think whatever you want, Hann. But you need to get used to it. As long as you're part of my life, I'll continue to protect you from anything or anyone who might hurt you."

"Apparently not everyone." She stared at me pointedly.

"What's that—"

"Never mind." She turned her back on me and stalked out of the cabin. When she was on the porch, she turned her head, and in a commanding tone I'd only ever heard come from Lydia, she said, "Make sure I get my messages from now on. I don't care if you think he or she is the next Charles Manson. If they call for me, I get the goddamned message, got it?"

"Fine." I held my hands up. "But it's not going to stop me from doing routine background checks on those I find suspicious."

"Dammit, Silas!" She turned all the way around, fire sparking in her emerald-green eyes. "I am not a child."

I let my gaze travel down to the neckline of her sundress, taking in the sweet swell of her breasts, and then I went lower, stopping at where the hem of her short dress hit her midthigh. "No, you most definitely are not." I licked my lips, trying and failing to quench the thirst I had for her.

She sucked in a short breath of air and flushed under my perusal.

So fucking gorgeous.

"Hannah!" I heard Wren call from outside the cabin, impatience ringing in his tone. "What the hell are you doing? The Jacksons are waiting to check in."

And untouchable.

Christ. Get ahold of yourself, man.

I cleared my throat and forced myself to meet her gaze. "No one ever said you were a child," I said quietly. "But you are a part of this family. And down here in the bayou, we take care of our own."

She completely ignored Wren and strode back into the cabin, stopping only when she was right in front of me. I fought hard to keep my hands to myself. Her proximity combined with the emotions swimming in her gaze was enough to break even the strongest man. But I held still, waiting.

That is until she placed her palm on my chest, lifted up on her tiptoes, and barely brushed her lips over mine.

"Hannah…," I breathed and dug my fingers into the flesh of her hips, warring with myself, unable to decide if I should physically remove her or pull her in tight until our bodies were molded together.

"Just one thing you should know," she whispered, her light wisteria scent intoxicating me. "About that mating thing?"

I raised one eyebrow, almost in challenge. "What about it?"

"We both know you want me. Want me so

bad you can taste it. And I'm here to tell you that by the end of this season… you're going to be begging me to let you bite me."

My dick went instantly hard. Fuck me. Had she really just said that?

My inner wolf clawed at the surface. Longed to take her, to claim her in every way. Heat seared me from the inside out until I thought I'd combust with desire right before her eyes. A vision of her on her hands and knees as I thrust into her from behind flashed through my mind… And then the bite. The one that would join us together forever. That would turn her wolf. Turn her into the very thing Lydia had never wanted for her daughter.

No. Dammit. No.

I suppressed a groan, released her, and took

a few steps back, reclaiming my personal space. Then I shook my head. "Don't say things like that, Hann. It's beneath you."

CHAPTER 3

HANNAH

THAT BASTARD. HIS words stung and were like a sucker punch to the gut. If he'd meant to embarrass me, he'd succeeded. My entire body was flushed with heat as I clenched my fists and stalked across the resort toward the front office. How dare he tell me what I should and shouldn't say? Or make me feel ashamed for voicing what had been brewing between us for years? I'd seen with my own two eyes what my words had done to him. His entire body had tensed and quivered with the effort to not touch me. Well, if he had so much freakin' self-control, then I was going to make him suffer.

A lot.

"Where have you been?" Wren asked, frowning at me from behind the front desk in the resort's office. "I was looking for you."

I ignored him as I walked over to the computer, tapped a few keys, and then typed out an e-mail to my friend Skye, the ex-model turned photographer.

Help. Need makeover and a shopping trip. STAT.

"Hannah?" Wren said again.

"What?" I sighed, irritated he was questioning me. Technically it was my day off, though he never seemed to realize I didn't actually work seven days a week. Due to his chef position up in New Orleans, he rarely put in any hours at the resort he co-owned with Silas and Darien.

"Were you with Silas again?" The reproach in his tone made something snap inside me.

"Jesus Christ, Wren. Yes. I was with Silas. Fucking his brains out." Adrenaline took over and my body shook from pure frustration.

He froze and his face went ghost-white in blind rage. "You... He... You didn't."

"No. Geez!" I threw my hands up. "Ever heard of sarcasm?"

He dropped his pen on the desk and stood up, disapproval swimming in his light gaze. "That's not funny."

"It wasn't meant to be," I shot back.

"For God's sake. He's your stepbrother.

Don't talk like that. What if a guest had heard you?"

I let out a loud groan of frustration. "No. He isn't. He never was. And I'm sick and tired of you trying to tell me what I can and can't do. So just back the hell off, all right?"

He stared at me openmouthed as he finally took a long look at me. Then he moved forward and stopped about a foot from me. "Uh, Hann?" he said hesitantly. "You're not acting like yourself. Did something happen today?"

"You think?" I snapped, not looking at him as I opened Skye's reply e-mail.

I'm free now. Want to come over?

I typed back immediately. *I'm on my way.*

Pulling my keys out of my handbag, I said, "Make sure the Jacksons get their tickets for the swamp tour. While you're there, find out if any of them have any food allergies so we can accommodate them for breakfast in the morning."

"You're leaving?" He stood up, blocking the door. "You can't leave. I have a date."

I glowered at him, and without another word, I stalked into Silas's private office and slipped out the back door.

"Are you sure about this?" I asked Skye as I stared in the mirror, trying not to grimace. I was used to wearing cotton dresses that, while cute, certainly weren't anything close to what one would classify as sexy.

Skye nodded, a gleam in her eye. "Hell yes.

If this doesn't make him crazy, nothing will."

"I just…" I tugged the top of the wraparound dress closer together. "I don't want to look slutty."

She laughed. "You? Slutty? Never. Listen, Hannah. This dress is classy. Maybe it's a little racy for the office, but since you don't work in a traditional setting, that's not going to be an issue. A little cleavage never hurt anyone. Not outside of a little sexual frustration anyway."

The dress was emerald green, cinched at the waist, and showed a heck of a lot more boobage and leg than I was normally comfortable with. It was just this side of tasteful with the hemline midthigh and the bodice showing off the goods without being indecent. "I don't know."

Skye shook her head, grabbed my hand, and pulled me out into her living room where her mate Jace and his brother Aiden were watching a NASCAR race.

"Well?" she said. "What do you think?"

I stood before them, feeling like I'd just walked into the classroom naked. The urge to cross my arms over my chest was overwhelming, but I forced myself to keep my hands at my sides. If I was going to play this game with Silas, I had to do it right. And that meant confidence. If I acted like a little girl playing dress-up, that's what he'd see and it would only make everything worse.

"Holy shit," Aiden said, his eyes wide and his eyebrows raised. "Is this Hannah?"

"Of course it is, you idiot," Jace said. Then he cast a glance at Skye. "Are you trying to kill him?"

She shrugged, totally unconcerned. "He

needs a wake-up call."

"He needs to get his head out of his ass," Aiden added.

"That too." Skye grinned and turned to me. "I think we've accomplished our mission. Come on. I'll hook you up with some more dresses."

With my face flushing from the unexpected praise, I followed her back into the bedroom and sat on the edge of her bed. She went straight to her closet and pulled out body-hugging dresses, low-rise jeans, and come-fuck-me pumps.

"Do not wear T-shirts with these." She held up a pair of skinny jeans. "Halter tops to show off those great shoulders of yours or blouses that give a peek at your cleavage, or heck, if you want to get crazy, a corset. Accent all your feminine features."

My anger had died and now I was starting to second-guess myself. "I'm not sure. This feels… manipulative. Like I'm resorting to the lowest common denominator."

"Oh, honey. Please. How often does he wander around the resort with no shirt on? You can't tell me he doesn't know what he's doing."

"It's hot out though."

"Right." She made a face and shoved the clothes in a tote bag. "And Darien or Wren? How often are they half-dressed around you?"

I pursed my lips, picturing them both. Jeans, T-shirts, and work boots. That was their normal uniform when they were there. Even when they were outside working. It wasn't that they never stripped down when they were overheated, but I couldn't even remember the last time I'd seen Silas fully clothed. Not unless he was leaving the compound.

"Give me the tote." I held my hand out, my resolve firmly in place. "You're right. It's time he had a taste of his own medicine."

"That's my girl." Skye shoved one more dress in the bag. "Wear that one when he's being particularly irritating." She winked and then walked me out.

"Are you sure this is okay?" I asked when we were standing next to my Honda Pilot.

"Of course. These are all things I used to wear when I was hired to model in high-end shoots. Around here, since I'm the photographer and outside so much of the time doing landscape shots, it's all about staying cool and comfy. Someone should put these to use."

"If you're sure," I said, but I was already climbing into my car.

"I'm sure." She laughed. "Now go knock him on his ass and call me to let me know how it goes."

"Will do." I waved as I sped off down the bayou road, my fingers gripped tightly around the steering wheel.

Silas Davenne wouldn't know what hit him.

CHAPTER 4
SILAS

The pounding of my feet on the hard-packed earth echoed in my ears. My breath came short, and sweat slicked my body. I'd been running for over five miles, and although my lungs and muscles were protesting, it wasn't enough. Not until the dull ache of fatigue drove Hannah's words from my mind.

Claiming her as my mate wasn't an option. If it was, I'd have done it long ago. I'd made a promise. Not to Wren, but to his mother. She hadn't wanted Hannah living life as a shifter.

She'd made that abundantly clear. More than once, and had made me promise to protect her from such a life.

There was a reason Lydia Valentine hadn't ever married my father even though they'd dated for over five years. She'd hated shifter life. Was scared of those always trying to uncover our secrets. Was scared for us and terrified we'd be taken from her. And despite loving us fiercely, she hadn't been able to handle my father's constant engagement with the local Hunters—a hate group that was always trying to expose us, or worse. And the day after a group of Hunters had burned down one of our cabins, she'd packed up and moved across the state.

She hadn't been able to get full custody of Wren, so he spent half his time with us and the other half with Lydia up in West Monroe. We'd heard she'd hooked up with someone new fairly quickly, and only a year later Hannah had been born. But Lydia had been careful to keep her little girl away from us. The last thing she wanted was her precious daughter getting mixed up with wolves.

The irony was that as soon as Lydia had passed five years ago, Hannah had come to live at Hidden Bayou because she hadn't had anywhere else to go. Her dad had skipped town years ago, and Wren was her only real family. And she didn't seem to care at all about shifter politics or her mother's wishes.

I loved her for it. More than I loved her for her sass or her sweetness or fierce determination. But I would not go against Lydia's wishes. No matter how she felt about the life of a shifter, she'd been the only parental figure who'd ever given a shit about me. Even after she left my father, she'd made it a priority to get in touch with me on a regular basis, to check in, to make sure we stayed connected. The fact that I hadn't actually seen her in eighteen years hadn't mattered. She'd always been available by phone when I'd needed someone.

Darien and I shared a biological mother. She'd left when Darien was two and I was only three months old. And our father... Well, he hadn't cared about much outside his motorcycle, gambling, and whatever woman was warming his bed. Mating hadn't been on his agenda. Too constricting, he'd said, but we all knew what he'd meant... He couldn't give up the party life. Or be mated to one woman forever.

I sped up, pushing harder as my wolf stirred

deep within me. The desire for family, for pack, for my mate… It took hold and wouldn't let go.

Letting out a low growl, I burst through the trees and sprinted up the steps to my cabin.

"Good workout?" Hannah's voice permeated my exercise haze.

I came to an abrupt stop, my hand clutching the doorknob on the front door. Because what I saw over in the corner of my porch took the last of my breath away. "Hannah?"

She rose gracefully from the porch swing. "I just came by to let you know the plumber's here working on a leak in cabin three."

I heard her words but didn't process a thing she said as my gaze fell to her exposed cleavage. The thin green fabric barely covered her peaches-and-cream flesh. A fire ignited inside me as images of the pair of us naked in my bed filled my mind. My entire body hardened, and I couldn't remember a time I wanted anything more.

"Silas?" she said, her tone uncertain.

"Jesus," I forced out, barely able to form words. But then I cleared my throat and said, "What the hell are you wearing?"

She let out a small huff. "It's called a dress. I'm certain you've been intimately familiar with one or two in your lifetime."

The impatience in her tone brought me up short, and I cut my gaze to hers.

She cocked one hip out to the side and raised her chin with indignation. "Finally. For a moment there I thought you forgot I had eyes."

"Hannah." I shook my head. "What are you doing?"

Her brows pinched together as she frowned,

irritation practically radiating off her. "I'm going out. Wren's working the office, but I wanted to let you know I'll be gone for the evening."

She was leaving? Wearing that?

Hell no. The words were right on the tip of my tongue, but I swallowed them. I couldn't demand she stay at the resort. She didn't belong to me, no matter how much I wished she did.

My muscles flexed and something primal in me longed to take her into my cabin and lock us both inside. If she'd been anyone else, I might have. If I hadn't made that promise so many years ago… Or if I didn't think she was too good for me.

Her heels clattered against my porch as she moved past me, her faint wisteria scent following her.

I reached out and grabbed her wrist, stopping her. "Hannah?"

She paused at the bottom of the step. "Yes?"

"Where are you going?"

She shook her head. "It doesn't matter. I'll see you in the morning."

I watched her walk away from me, her hips swaying gently in the body-hugging dress. "Girls' night out? You headed to Skye's?"

She paused once more, stared me straight in the eyes, and said, "No. I have a date."

"A date?" I said stupidly, frozen in shock.

"Yes, a date," she echoed. "Maybe you've heard of it. You know, when a man asks a woman out. Dinner's usually involved. Maybe some dancing. And if all goes well, maybe I'll invite him back to my place."

"Your place!" My voice boomed as I leaped

off the porch and yanked her to me. Circling her waist with one arm, I buried my hand in her hair and brought my lips inches from hers. There was a deep growl in my voice when I spoke. "Do not bring him here."

"Why?" Her eyes were narrowed in challenge.

"You know why."

She shook her head. "Say it, Silas. Tell me why I can't bring my date here."

"Fuck." My fingers curled into her hair as I tightened my grip. "Because you're mine, Hannah. You always have been. And you always will be. You know what will happen if you bring someone else here."

Her eyelashes lowered as she gazed at my mouth, hunger straining in the soft quiver of her body against mine. "Then show me."

CHAPTER 5
Hannah

My breath left me as my heart slammed against my ribs. The tension sparking between us was charged with so much energy we both vibrated with it.

Silas sucked in a sharp breath and took a half step back, loosening his grip on me.

I pressed my lips together in a thin line, my perpetual frustration with him nearing the boiling point. "This right here"—I waved a hand between us—"the fact that you are once again pulling away from me, is why I'm definitely not yours. And I'll be damned if I wait for you for even one more minute."

"You know we can't go down this path." Despite his words, Silas's hand tightened on my waist. Talk about mixed signals.

I tore from his grasp and stalked toward the trees that lined the parking lot. "Forget it, Silas. I'm done with this."

"There isn't a *this*," I heard him say as he stormed back up onto the front porch of his cabin.

"Clearly!" I yelled, not looking back. Angry tears sprang to my eyes as I ran to my car. And when I saw my reflection in the window, I shook my head at the ridiculous way I'd tried to get his attention. The dress, my hair, the extra makeup. It wasn't me. None of it. And while Skye had only been trying to help, my sophisticated makeover designed to drive Silas crazy had been a mistake.

I had half a mind to turn back to my own cabin, to change my clothes, but I couldn't face seeing anyone. I had to get out of there. Not that I had anywhere to go. There was no date. Silas had already seen to that when he'd done a background check on Colin. Not that I'd really wanted to go out with him either. I'd only had eyes for Silas for the past six years. No one else had ever come close.

"Shit," I muttered and cranked the ignition of my Honda. I had to get away. Had to get my head back on straight.

Silas emerged from the tree line, his hands stuffed in his pockets and shoulders hunched forward.

I waited a half beat for him to make a signal

for me to stop, to move toward me, to call out, to do anything. But when he remained still, only watching me, I let out a loud huff and stepped on the gas. The gravel sprayed from beneath my tires as I shot out of the parking lot, refusing to look back.

Forget him.

I wasn't going to live my life waiting for something that was never going to come. It was time to move on.

The trees blurred in my peripheral vision as I sped away from the bayou, intending to head straight into New Orleans. Just because I didn't have a date didn't mean I couldn't go looking for one. I had friends in the city who'd be more than happy to go bar-hopping with me.

My phone buzzed on the seat beside me, followed by the ringing through the stereo system via my Bluetooth. Silas's name popped up on my media console.

I scowled and hit Decline. He was too late.

Then I hit Thea's name and gripped the steering wheel harder while it rang.

"Hey, Hannah. Long time no talk," she said. "What's going on?"

"I'm headed into town. Are you up for going out for a few drinks?"

She laughed. "Always. Meet me at Martine's, say forty minutes?"

"Perfect. See you then… And, Thea?"

"Yeah?"

"Don't let me leave without a hot guy on my arm." The very thought of getting close to someone who wasn't Silas left an uneasy pit in my gut. But I had to do something or it was very possible I'd end up pining for him for the rest of my life.

"You're serious?"

"Yes." The conviction in my tone surprised even me.

"You got it. I know the perfect guy. He's just your type: tall, dark, and dangerous. Kinda broody too."

I stifled a groan and forced cheer into my tone. "He sounds perfect."

"You have no idea." She laughed, and then the line went dead.

"Will just walked in," Thea said into her beer, her long brunette hair falling forward over her face.

I cut my gaze over my shoulder and spotted

a tall, muscular guy with dark features and olive skin. He moved gracefully, almost catlike with his large frame. Sexy. Too sexy to be single. "What's wrong with him?"

"You're kidding, right? Nothing." Her eyes went gooey as she stared at him.

I handed her a napkin. "You might want to wipe that drool off your chin."

"Oh, shut up." She swatted my hand away.

"Seriously. What's wrong with him? No one that gorgeous is ever single. And if they are, that usually means they either have commitment issues or they play for the other team."

She lifted one eyebrow. "Like Silas? Which is he?"

"Commitment issues for sure," I mumbled, fully aware that his misguided sense of honor was the real problem. "I'm not looking for a project. I already have one of those."

She nodded solemnly. "I hear that. But don't worry. He's just new in town. If you don't snag him now, he'll be taken by the end of the month."

I didn't doubt her. If he had even rudimentary social skills, the women would be throwing themselves at him before they even got him to pay for dinner. He was that good-looking. "And why haven't you already tried to snag him?"

"Because I just started seeing someone last month." She cast me a side-eye glance and gave me a silly grin. "It's still new and exciting, only…" She let out a long-suffering sigh. "I'm not sure it's going anywhere."

"At least you're actually dating."

"Sure. If you call sleeping together 'dating.' He's yet to take me out on a real date."

"Oh, Thea," I said, sympathy in my tone. "Why are you putting up with that?"

Tucking a lock of hair behind her ear, she shrugged. "I like the time we spend together. But if it doesn't change soon, I'll have to drop his sexy ass." She winked and waved at Will, casting him her infectious smile.

He gave her a short nod, almost business-like, and wove his way through the crowd toward us. Just as he reached the bar, he swept his steely blue eyes over me. A small, appreciative smile played over his lips while he drank me in, obvious approval in his expression.

I struggled to keep the smile on my face. There was something about him, something I couldn't put my finger on, that instantly made me wary.

"Will, this is Hannah. My friend I told you

about," Thea said.

He held out his hand, meeting my gaze. "It's a pleasure to finally meet you."

I raised both eyebrows as I quickly shook his hand. "Finally?"

His smile twisted into something that seemed more creepy than inviting. I pulled my hand away, the unease in my gut spreading. But then just like that, his smile was gone and intelligence shone back at me from his eyes. "Thea mentioned you the first night I got to town. I was wondering when I'd get a chance to put a face to the name."

Seriously? I glanced between them, trying to read Thea. I'd met her two years ago in my last semester of college, and although I called her a friend, we only saw each other once every couple of months. For her to be mentioning me to a stranger right off just seemed odd.

"I was talking about that time we sweet-talked our way into riding in that Mardi Gras parade. Remember how you told that one guy you were starring in the next *Hunger Games* movie?" She laughed. "It worked like a charm."

Will grinned. "I like a resourceful woman."

My shoulders relaxed as I laughed at the memory. The guy had been so drunk he'd spent the night referring to me as Katniss. It was a small price to pay for admittance on the float.

"Let me buy you a drink," Will said, already flagging the bartender down.

Thea's smile widened, and then she slipped off the barstool and backed away, waving her fingers at me as she went.

I opened my mouth to stop her, but Will dropped one arm over my shoulder and pulled me into his body as if we were on a date and hadn't just met a minute before. "Whoa, buddy," I said, trying to keep my tone light. "Maybe we should get to know each other a little before you start clutching me."

He laughed and let go just as the music level ratcheted up to almost unbearable. "Sure, sweetheart," he called over the music, moving to stand behind me. Then he lowered his head to my ear and said, "Let's go outside where we can talk a little easier."

Before I could protest, he moved forward, herding me through the ever-growing crowd toward the front door. I debated stepping to the side or causing a scene but decided the bar was so totally not where I wanted to be and once we got outside, I'd just make an excuse and get the hell out of there. I hadn't really wanted a date.

I'd only wanted Silas to think I did.

The warm spring air engulfed us as we stepped out into the humidity on a quiet side street in uptown, just two blocks from the university. I took a few steps away, held up my phone, and said, "I'm sorry, but my brother just sent a text and something's come up at home. I'm going to need to get back."

Will frowned, disappointment flashing over his expression. "Really? But I kinda hoped we'd get to talk for a minute."

"Sorry," I said again and took another step back. "Emergency."

"Looks like they're going to have to manage without you," another voice said in my ear just as two strong arms wrapped around me from behind and lifted me off my feet.

"Hey!" I cried, kicking back at whoever was

manhandling me, my heart thumping wildly against my ribcage. "What the hell are you doing?"

"Following orders," he said.

"Will!" I cried, desperate for some help. But Thea's friend just nodded once at the person gripping me and slipped back into the bar, leaving me alone on the street with the stranger.

"Help!" I cried at the top of my lungs, my nails digging into the man's arms. "Rape!"

"Shut the fuck up," the man said, his tone sharp, followed by a large hand covering my mouth.

I chomped down on his palm, biting as hard as I could.

"Fucking bitch!" The man pulled his hand away while at the same time dragging me backward toward a car I hadn't seen when we'd first come out of the bar. "Fight me again and I'll break your goddamned arm."

I ignored his threats. My self-defense education came roaring back and my teacher's voice rang in my head. *Do whatever it takes to get away. The risk of fatality goes up significantly once your attacker has you isolated.*

I was not getting in that car. He'd have to kill me on the street first.

The man whipped me around and lunged forward, trying to stuff me into the car. I threw my feet out in front of me, bracing myself against the doorframe, using my legs to keep him from tossing me inside.

"You stupid—"

I threw my head back and heard the sickening crunch of bone on bone followed by a loud roar. We fell to the ground, my attacker crying out but still unwilling to let me go. Dammit. He wasn't giving up. I rolled and the man rolled with me, coming up on top of me, his nose spilling blood all over my dress.

"You're going to pay for that," he spat, saliva and blood splattering on my face.

"Get off me!"

He grinned, evil flashing in his bloodshot eyes as he picked my arm up and then slammed it right back down onto the ground. It hit something at an angle, and a loud snap sounded in my ear, followed by intense pain shooting from my wrist all the way up to my shoulder.

I screamed, immobilized by the pain as the edges of my vision turned black.

Then I heard a loud grunt and suddenly the man was off me.

I cradled my arm against my chest and

peered up at the familiar stance of... Silas? I squinted, wondering if I was hallucinating.

He had his back to me and was stalking forward.

My attacker was on the ground, scrambling to his feet, his eyes darting between me and Silas.

But before Silas could get another punch off, the guy turned and sprinted down the street. Silas took off after him but then stopped abruptly and turned to look at me. "Hannah? Are you okay?"

I shook my head, tears standing in my eyes. "I think it's broken." I nodded toward my throbbing wrist.

"That bastard." He cast a quick glance down the street. The man was already gone. Only his car remained. Silas pulled his phone out and started tapping the screen. But then another car rounded the corner and came to a sudden stop next to us.

I took a step back, unconsciously pressing into Silas's chest as I met the narrowed gaze of the familiar driver. Will. And in the back seat, pounding on the window, was Thea.

"Oh my God!" I ran forward, intending to yank the door open, but Will stepped on the gas, making the tires squeal as the car shot forward. "Silas! He has my friend. We have to go after them."

He didn't hesitate. With his arm wrapped around my shoulders, he steered me toward his black Jeep, half parked on the sidewalk behind my attacker's car. After hastily helping me into the passenger's seat, he ran around to the driver's side, and before he even got his door shut we were on our way.

I gritted my teeth against the throbbing pain in my arm and hunched forward, scanning the street for the dark blue Chevy. "That way," I said, jerking my head to the right.

Silas swerved and I slid to the side, slamming into the door. "Ouch!"

He grimaced. "Shit. Sorry, Hannah."

I shook my head, trying to ignore the sudden bout of nausea. "Don't worry about me. We need to find Thea."

"Do you know who she's with?"

"His name is Will. Thea said he was a friend of hers, but after what went down… God. No way."

"And what about that guy's nose you smashed?" He sent me a small smile, pride glinting in his dark eyes.

"No idea. But they're working together. Will led me outside and I was going to leave, but then that bastard attacked me. Will just took off back into the bar. To get Thea obviously."

"Fucking pieces of shit," Silas said under his breath and sped up, following the Chevy around a tight corner. The back end of his Jeep fishtailed slightly, but Silas quickly got the vehicle under control, and a second later, we were gaining on the blue car.

It was almost pitch-black on the street we were barreling down, and it wasn't one I recognized, though that wasn't a surprise since I spent most of my time down in the bayou. But it was obvious we were in a part of town that didn't welcome outsiders. The cars that were parked on the street had their tires stripped, and from what I could see, there were bars on the windows of the small, run-down homes.

Silas likely didn't have any qualms, considering he was a former Marine and a wolf. But me? I was just a human with a few days self-defense training. Even if my wrist weren't broken, I would likely only last two minutes on my own. None of that would've stopped me from going after Thea though. She was my friend, and one way or another we were going to bring her home.

"Check the glove box," Silas ordered.

I cast a quick glance at him. "Why?"

"My nine millimeter's in there. The only way we're going to get this guy to stop is to blow his tires."

"Right." I pulled up on the latch and the glove box swung open. Just as he said, right inside was a small black handgun. I pulled it out and handed it to him, knowing I'd never get a straight shot off with my left hand. Had my right one been whole, I'd already have been leaning out the window, bringing that asshole down.

"Can you hold the wheel?" Silas asked, palming the gun.

I nodded, reached over and grabbed it with my left hand. And then, just as Silas shifted to lean out the window, another car came out of nowhere and slammed into my side of the Jeep. The sound of broken glass combined with the crumpling of metal and fiberglass filled my awareness, and the world moved in a blur around us.

Then all at once we hit something head-on and came to an abrupt stop.

There was no sound. No movement. Just the ringing of destruction playing in my ears.

Blinking, I turned my head and met Silas's horrified stare.

"Are you hurt?" I managed to force out, though my chest had tightened and I was finding it hard to breathe.

"Hannah." His voice was strained, and for the first time in my life, I saw something I'd never seen in Silas's expression.

Fear.

CHAPTER 6

SILAS

TERROR SEIZED ME and something vital deep in my chest broke wide-open. Emotion rose up and choked me as I stared at Hannah. At the piece of metal sticking out of her chest.

Her eyes were glassy, clouded over with shock. But she still managed to ask, "Are you okay?"

"I'm fine, love," I whispered, having no idea what kind of condition I was in. It didn't matter. I'd heal. My wolf blood would take over, and by the next day I'd be fine.

But Hannah wouldn't. There was no time to get her to the hospital. Not with the way she was already fading. Her faint heartbeat was slowing and the scent of her blood filled the Jeep. She was moments from slipping from our world.

"Hannah," I choked out.

Her eyes fluttered as she gazed up at me, barely able to focus. "My wrist doesn't hurt anymore."

I glanced at her arm lying at an odd angle and felt my stomach roll. "Dammit, no, Hannah. You can't leave like this."

"I'm right here," she said, her voice barely a whisper as her lids slid closed.

"Oh God." My insides were being ripped out. I reached for her, pulling her body to me. "Hannah, sweetheart."

She let out a low moan and a trickle of blood ran from the corner of her mouth.

She was dying and I had no choice. It was now or never. "Open your eyes," I ordered.

Her head rolled slightly to the side and her lids twitched, indicating she'd heard me. But movement was obviously too much for her.

"I need to know you understand what I'm about to say. Make a sound."

Another small moan.

"Listen, love. I'm going to bite you now. Turn you wolf. I need you to accept it. Willfully. Can you do that for me?"

This time her eyes did open. "Mate," she mouthed.

"Yes. I'm going to make you my mate."

Her lips twitched into a tiny, small smile as her head rolled again.

There was no choice. No real thought other than I couldn't lose her. Not now. Not ever. With a low growl and my chest aching as if I would explode, I lowered my head and bit into the smooth area of her neck. A small trickle of her blood seeped into my mouth, but as I lapped at the wounds, they began to heal under my administrations.

Her body was so still, so cold, I began to think I'd been too late. Her neck was healing, but was my wolf magic strong enough to heal the massive damage the rest of her body had suffered?

While I held her, I reached into my pocket and grabbed my phone. With one touch, the phone was ringing.

"Smoke here," Devon, a member of our pack who was living in New Orleans, said after the second ring.

"Can you track my location?"

"Sure. It's already up on my screen. What are you doing in the city?" Smoke was a hacker and all-around computer genius. He took care of the security for the resort and my cousin's bar. Locating my cell phone was child's play for him.

"Hannah and I have been in a bad accident. I need you to come get us. Fast, before the first responders get here."

"I'm on my way." The line went dead.

I glanced around at the dark street, marveling that neither the cops nor an ambulance had been called. Though judging by the almost deserted neighborhood, it appeared the residents either kept to themselves or were under orders to ignore us. It was likely the latter.

Whoever had hit us had already disappeared, leaving us alone in an abandoned lot.

It was just as well. Even in the darkness, I could see Hannah's scrapes and bruises already starting to heal. My magic was working. Explaining that to an emergency room doctor would be awkward at best. At worst, she'd end up as a lab rat.

Hell no. I'd never let that happen.

"Silas," Hannah said, taking in a sharp breath. "Ugh." Her face crumpled with pain, and she started to curl in on herself.

I placed a hand on her shoulder, keeping her down. "Don't move. It'll only make it worse."

"It feels like someone staked me in the chest." Her fingers twitched as if she was going to reach for whatever it was she felt, but I slipped my fingers between hers and lightly held her in place.

"Shhh," I soothed. "Everything's going to be all right. Smoke's on his way, and soon we'll have you in a safe house where I can tend to your wounds."

"Safe house?" Her brow crinkled, but before I could answer, she let out a loud cry and thrashed in my arms.

"Hang on, Hannah," I said, reaching for the mangled glove box, desperately trying to yank the thing open. "Son of a bitch," I muttered and grabbed the entire thing, trying to rip it right out of the dash.

"Silas!" Hannah reached for me, her entire body shaking. Her skin was damp and her heart was now racing.

I stared down into her wild eyes and knew if

she'd gained enough strength, she was moments from shifting.

"Hold on," I ordered and kicked the driver's side door open. "Not here." Not anywhere if I could help it. Not yet anyway. If she shifted with that metal stuck in her, it would be excruciating.

Her breathing became rapid and her skin hot. She'd gone from ice-cold to developing a fever in less than three minutes. If only I could get the painkillers from my glove box.

"We have to get you out of here," I said and unceremoniously pulled her out of the Jeep, gritting my teeth against her cry of agony. "I'm so sorry," I said over and over again as I cradled her to my chest. "Just another minute."

Shaking her head violently, she struggled in my arms. "I can't. Let me down."

"Not yet. We need to get you to Smoke's place." Headlights shone at the end of the street and the car sped up, heading right toward us. "He's almost here."

"I can't—" She let out a loud gasp, and then before I could stop her, she grabbed the metal still sticking in her chest with both hands. With a roar of determination, she yanked it out. Blood seeped over her chest and dripped to the ground.

"Jesus Christ, Hannah!" I laid her on the ground, ripped my shirt off, and pressed it to her gaping wound.

Her breathing, while still a little rough, returned to normal. But she was once again ghost-white. "The pressure… too much."

The car squealed to a stop beside us, and in an instant Scarlett, Smoke's mate, was out of the car and kneeling beside me. "What happened?"

"Car crash. She was too far gone. I had to do something…" I paused, unable to get the words out.

"You turned her?" Scarlett asked in a matter-of-fact tone.

"I had to. No choice."

Scarlett met Smoke's gaze for about half a beat and then nodded. "Looks like you saved her life."

"Here." Smoke handed her a syringe. "This will put her out while she heals."

"No," Hannah said, shaking her head. "I have questions."

I gently placed my hand over her brow and leaned in. "It's okay, love. I'll be right by your side when you wake up."

"You promise?" The fear and wistfulness in her tone broke my heart all over again. Even as she lay there in more pain than I could ever imagine, she was questioning my loyalty to her.

"I promise. I'll never leave your side again if that's what you want."

She raised the arm that hadn't been broken and curled her scraped-up fingers around my arm. "Never again," she whispered.

"Never again," I echoed and then gestured to Scarlett, indicating now was the time.

Scarlett pressed her lips together, tested the syringe, and then slid the needle into Hannah's thigh. Within moments, Hannah's head listed to the side and all the tension left her body. Scarlett pressed her fingers to Hannah's pulse and nodded. "She's out. Let's get her out of here."

Smoke moved to help me, but I brushed him aside and lifted my mate into my arms. "Take us somewhere I can tend her wounds and then lie with her until she wakes up."

Smoke nodded. "You got it."

CHAPTER 7

HANNAH

My body felt heavy, as if something was weighing me down. Vague shadows and unidentifiable images ran through my mind as I struggled to form some sort of coherent thought.

"Hannah?"

I stirred, Silas's deep voice penetrating my haze.

"Wake up, love. I'm right here."

I pried my eyes open and blinked.

Silas smiled down at me. "Welcome back."

I opened my mouth to speak, but the words got caught in my dry throat.

"Here." Silas produced a glass of water complete with a straw.

I opened my mouth and sucked down a long pull of water, reveling in the cool liquid. "Thank you," I said as I glanced around at the unfamiliar bedroom. The walls were standard beige, but the ceiling was at least twelve feet high and the floors hardwood. And the window looked out on a wrought iron balcony. A vague recollection of the night's events flashed in my mind, and a shiver ran down my spine. Then I sat straight up. "Thea. Where is she?"

Silas reached up and circled my wrist with his fingers. "Smoke is doing everything he can to trace her whereabouts. The moment he knows anything, he'll let us know."

I glanced around, frantic. "But she was taken. Right? That's what happened?" My memories were fuzzy, but I was pretty sure I hadn't dreamed that.

"She was. And we'll find her, too. One way or another. Smoke won't let us down."

I sat there, my insides churning. "We have to do something more. *I* have to do something."

"Hann, you already are. You're healing, regaining your strength after the accident. It's the best thing you can do right now."

I sucked in a hard breath as the accident came roaring back in flashes of confusion. I squeezed my eyes shut, doing my best to block it out. When I opened them again, I focused on his steely eyes. "Where are we?"

"A house in the Lower Garden District." Silas tugged me back down and curled into me.

I stiffened, realizing for the first time I wasn't wearing anything more than a skimpy tank top and cotton panties.

Silas froze. "Are you all right? Did I hurt you? Does your chest still hurt?"

"What? No. I—" Crap. Had I really had a piece of metal in my chest? I lifted the cover and glanced down at myself. My skin was as smooth as it ever was. Not a scar in sight.

"It's the wolf blood," Silas said quietly, wrapping his arm around my center and tucking me in close to him.

"Wolf blood?" I asked, wondering if I'd had some sort of transfusion. Beyond the metal debris being lodged in my chest, everything else was vague.

"Yes. It healed you." His clean, soapy scent filled my senses. And just like that, all other thoughts flew from my mind. How I'd survived the car wreck didn't matter. Not when Silas was in bed next to me and I was wearing almost nothing, my back pressed up against his chest, his hand splayed on my bare stomach.

I swallowed. "Uh, Silas?"

"Yes, love?" He nuzzled my neck with soft kisses.

My blood heated and my pulse quickened. "What's happening here?"

He pushed himself up on one elbow, rolled me over onto my back, and stared down at me. "I told you I'd be here when you woke up."

"And so you are," I said, trying to be neutral, but his close proximity and the fact that we were in bed together suddenly had my hormones working overtime. It was all I could do to not grab him by the shirt, yank him down, and devour him.

His eyes narrowed slightly. "How much do you remember?"

I shook my head. "Not much. The other car slamming into us. Then it's mostly confusion."

"Oh, Hannah," he breathed and brushed a lock of hair off my cheek. "I guess it's better you don't remember. It was pretty bad."

"How bad?"

Something unreadable flashed through his eyes before he lay down on his back beside me and tugged me over, positioning me so my head was resting on his chest. With both arms wrapped around me, he started running his fingers through my hair.

I took a deep breath. "I almost died, didn't I?" I already knew my words word true. My skewering aside, we were in bed together with me barely dressed. And he was holding me tight, seemingly unwilling to let me go. So unlike him.

"Yes." A muscle in his neck pulsed and I had to fight to keep from kissing it. Now was not the time.

"And you gave me wolf blood?"

He sucked in a sharp breath and sat up, taking me with him. The covers fell and the cool air-conditioning made gooseflesh pop out over my skin. I instantly crossed my arms over my chest and rubbed my shoulders with my palms.

"You don't remember, do you?" Silas said, his voice strained.

I shook my head. "Everything's a blur. I remember the impact, then nothing until a pain that was utterly unbearable seized me, and I felt like I was going to come right out of my skin.

But it's all very faint. Almost dreamlike."

"Shit." He ran a frustrated hand through his short dark hair.

"Silas. What is it?" I asked, yanking the sheet up to cover myself.

"Dammit. This isn't the way this was supposed to happen." He climbed out of the bed and paced.

The loss was immediate. Almost as if a part of me had been ripped away. Physical pain blossomed in my chest, leaving me gasping for air. "Silas?"

He didn't stop the pacing.

"Silas!"

He paused and glanced at me, his tattooed arms rippling with tension.

I reached out for him. "Please. I just need you to hold me for another few minutes."

He swept his gaze over me, seeming to drink me in. Then without another word, he reached behind his neck and pulled his T-shirt over his head.

I pitched forward on the bed and rose up on my knees, unable to keep myself from touching him. As soon as my hands flattened against his hard chest, the pain vanished. I let out a small satisfied sigh and leaned into him.

He barely breathed, letting me press soft kisses against his lips.

The question was right there in the back of my mind. Why wasn't he running like he usually did? But I didn't care. Not even if the answer was pity. I physically needed him and wasn't ashamed to show him just how much.

"Kiss me back, Silas," I ordered.

I could somehow feel his arousal as if it

were my own. It hit me hard and lit something primal within me.

His eyes turned molten, and then with a growl he covered my mouth with his and kissed me with a fiery passion that made my toes curl. I melted into him and got lost in the insistent thrusts of his tongue running over mine.

It was everything I remembered and more. Hot. Intoxicating. Thorough. And also intense, magical, and devastating. Everything about it was perfect and my heart swelled, knowing without a doubt he was *mine*.

"Make me yours, Silas," I gasped out. "Do it now."

He gazed down at me, his eyes burning with need. Then he let out a low, ironic chuckle. "Are you sure that's what you want?"

I nodded and ran my hands down his chest,

my fingers lingering on his ripped abs.

"Just like that? You'd let me turn you? What about Wren?" He grabbed my wrists and encircled me, pinning both my arms behind my back.

I arched into him, exposing my neck, more than ready to put this dance behind us. "Yes, I will. I want you. I always have. And you know it."

"But your family doesn't want this for you," he said and lowered his mouth to my collarbone. Gently, he scraped his teeth over my skin, making me shiver with tortured anticipation.

I steeled myself and straightened, needing my head to be clear for this conversation. "Which family? My mother? She never wanted the shifter life because of your father. He never loved her the way a man is supposed to love a woman. Because if there's one thing I know about my mom—she wanted an all-consuming love. One that transcended time and place and common sense. I can guarantee if she'd had that with your father, she would've never left. She spent her life looking for it. And never found it."

Silas swallowed, his dark gaze searching mine. "Is that what you think is between us?"

I stared back, getting lost in the tumultuous storm raging in the depths of his eyes. He'd just asked the question that if I answered would lay me wide-open. Expose my deepest desire. Leave me stripped bare, vulnerable. "Yes."

His eyes drifted closed for just a moment as he took a deep breath. "And what about Wren?"

"What about him?" Anger flared to life and

it was all I could do to keep from screaming. "He has no say in this. It's between you and me. And I think I've made myself perfectly clear."

Silas's lips curved slightly, then he bent and kissed me. His lips brushed over mine, soft and gentle, a whisper of what was to come. Then he released my wrists and buried one hand in my hair while the other cupped my cheek. "Tell me you want to be my mate, Hannah."

I raised my hands, placing them on either side of his face, and then held his gaze. "I have been waiting for you to make me your mate for six years. Don't you think we've both suffered enough?"

His eyes glinted with satisfaction. "Yes. We have."

Triumph and joy exploded within me. Finally he'd said the words I'd been waiting so long to hear.

"Only I have something to tell you first."

Son of a… My stomach dropped straight to my toes. I'd been an idiot to get my hopes up. "Dammit, Silas. If you give me some other bullshit reason—"

He pressed his fingers to my lips. "Shh. It's not like that."

I sat back down on the bed, suddenly exhausted. "Then tell me what it's like."

The bed shifted as he sat beside me, his large arm tucking me against him. "I should've told you straight off, but I had to know how you really feel. I had to know if this was your choice before we went any further."

I sighed. "I don't know how I could've made myself any clearer." I glanced down at my thin tank top. "Did you not notice the green dress that barely covered all this?" I waved a hand in front of my chest.

He groaned. "Oh, I noticed all right. Were you trying to kill me?"

"Yes. As a matter of fact, I was."

He chuckled. "You almost succeeded." Sobering, he took my hand in both of his. "Listen. The crash. It was bad. Really fucking bad."

I nodded, knowing what he said was true, even though my memory was shot to hell.

"You…" He swallowed. "There was a piece of metal in your chest. The only way you could survive was if you had wolf blood."

My heart started pounding, and I squeezed his hand, already knowing what he was going to say. It was so obvious. Should've been the first thing I thought of when I'd woken up without so much as a scratch.

"I had no choice. Feeding you my blood would never have been enough. The injuries were too great. I had to turn you. To make you my mate." He lowered his lashes, unable to look at me, as if he were ashamed.

"Silas?" My voice was quiet.

"Yeah?" he murmured, still not looking at me.

"You saved my life."

He nodded and raised his head, meeting my gaze. "I'd do it again in a heartbeat. No one could stop me. But dammit. It was the last thing I wanted to do."

A cool sweat broke out over my body and doubt started to creep into my consciousness. He'd turned me because he had to. But now that I was his, did he want me? "Do you regret it?"

His eyes narrowed. "No."

"I don't mean because you didn't want me to die. I'm talking about the fact that I'm now your mate. Your choice was taken from you, and you're stuck with me."

"Stuck?" He raised both his eyebrows in surprise. Then he let out a loud laugh. "Stuck?" he asked again.

I pressed my lips together and glared at him. "This isn't funny."

He shook his head, sobering. "No. It isn't. Listen. The only thing I regret about claiming you as my mate is that I didn't get to do it while making love to you. Do you have any idea how many different ways I've imagined this moment? Not one of them included watching the life drain from your gorgeous green eyes."

Relief and elation surged through me. He'd

only confirmed what I'd always known. And although I'd never willingly choose to get my way by almost dying, I certainly wasn't going to regret the outcome. "How many ways?"

His expression turned heated, wolfish, and that primal thing deep inside me stirred again. Need, passion, hunger. It boiled just beneath the surface, and before I could stop it, a low rumbling growl erupted from the back of my throat.

Silas's gaze shifted to my mouth and his muscles bunched as if he was straining to hold himself back. Then in one swift movement, he lifted me up off the bed and settled me so I was straddling his lap. "You want me." His words were a statement of fact, no challenge, no judgment. Only a confirmation. "Tell me what you need."

"All of you. Everywhere. Skin on skin, on top of me, under me, behind me."

"Jesus," he said, already pulling my tank top up and cupping one breast with his hand.

"And I want your mouth on me, your tongue everywhere, and then"—I ground into him—"I want you inside me, making me yours once and for all."

"Fuck," he murmured, squeezing my ass with his free hand.

I dug my nails into his shoulders and arched my back, silently begging for him to put his mouth on me.

He didn't disappoint. Taking my cue, he dipped his tongue into my cleavage and teased my nipple with his thumb and forefinger.

A shot of pure pleasure sent heat between my legs. I was so turned on that I pulsed with need so intense I thought I'd die if he didn't touch me there. "Silas," I begged and rocked into him. "Please."

"No. Not yet. I've waited too long for this." He lifted me off him and placed me on my feet. Grinning, he stood and ran his hands up my sides, taking the tank top off over my head. We were both bare from the waist up. Only I was at a disadvantage in my underwear while he still wore his jeans.

"Take them off," I said, casting my eyes down at the obtrusive denim.

He shook his head and slid his hands down my hips, slipping his fingers into the scrap of cotton I wore. His touch was light, cool, and unbearable. I trembled with the gentleness of his fingers.

"So fucking perfect," he whispered as his

pupils dilated with need.

"I will be once I get you inside me," I shot back and reached for the button on his jeans.

He just stood there with a ghost of a smile while I divested him of his jeans and boxers. Once I stepped back, he kicked his clothes to the side as I licked my lips.

Holy Christ. He was gorgeous. His vibrant tattoos covered both arms, but the rest of him was unmarked. His wide chest was cut and his waist narrow as if he worked out at the gym every day. But I knew better. It was from all the physical labor.

I reached out, letting my fingers trail down to his V cut, and shuddered with anticipation. Damn, I was a complete goner.

"Hannah?" His voice was strained.

"Yeah?" I glanced up at him, barely able to

take my eyes off his perfect body.

"I will stand here as long as you want me to, but you might want to know that the longer you touch me like that, the more likely it is I'm going to lose my fucking mind."

I grinned. "Good."

But then he grabbed me and lifted me up. My legs automatically curled around his waist as he claimed my lips. Our tongues met as he spun me around and lowered me to the bed. Never once breaking the kiss, he nudged my legs open with one knee and settled between my thighs, his hard shaft pressing against my hip.

"Whoa," I said, my breathing already rapid. "This just took a giant step forward."

"It's just the beginning, love. I'm going to show you at least four of my different fantasies before we finish this."

"Four?" Anticipation coiled in my gut.

"Uh-huh." Threading his fingers between mine, he moved my hands above my head and pressed them into the soft mattress. "This is number one."

"What—oh!"

His mouth was on my breast again, only this time he sucked my nipple in and bit down just hard enough to evoke a delicious mix of pleasure and pain. I whimpered, aching for more.

"Make that sound again," Silas ordered as he dipped his head, giving attention to my other breast.

I gasped and pulled my hands out of his grip, aching to touch him, to be an active participant in the moment. And when I dug my fingers into his shoulders, he moved his hands to my sides while trailing kisses down my abdomen. When he got to my hip, he glanced up at me. "Are you ready for this?"

"Yes," I answered, breathless, the pulsing between my thighs reaching mind-numbing levels.

And then his mouth was on me, his tongue hot and insistent against my flesh.

"Oh, God," I said and dug my fingers into his short hair, already coming undone.

He moved and hit just the right spot while simultaneously plunging two fingers inside me. He thrust once, twice, and then I cried out, my muscles clenching around him as the orgasm hit me hard. It crashed through me, wave after wave as Silas kept his mouth on me, taking me to a place of pure ecstasy.

He rode it out with me, stroking and laving until the quivers stopped and my body stilled.

"Whoa," he said with a chuckle in his tone when he finally came up for air.

"You can say that again," I agreed, unable to even move, my muscles liquid.

"Oh no you don't." He crawled his way back up the bed and lay beside me, his hands already roving over my body. "We're not even close to being done here."

"That's good news." I smiled at him and then sobered when I saw the determination shining back at me in his eyes.

"That was only number one." He raised an eyebrow in challenge.

"I'm not going anywhere." That was the last thing I wanted to do. His callused hand was rough against my sensitive skin, and I was once again tingling with need. In fact, the longer I watched him, the more my inner wolf rose to the surface, wanting to claim him. Make him mine in every way.

Something came over me and suddenly I was no longer the inexperienced one waiting for Silas to call the shots. I needed him. Now.

I rolled, pushing him down on his back as I straddled him.

"You have a plan, Hannah?" he asked, his tone playful.

"Only one."

"And what's that?"

I smiled down at him. "To take you deep inside me and make you come so hard you nearly pass out."

His hands tightened on my thighs as his expression turned to one of pure hunger. "Well, what are you waiting for?"

CHAPTER 8
SILAS

Hannah leaned down, her round, firm breasts pressing against my bare chest, and trailed hot kisses down my neck until she got to the hollow at my throat. Then she used her tongue, flicking it over my skin.

I tilted my head back, giving her full access. Jesus, she was passionate. Greedy. And made me so hard I was just about ready to lose control. Not one of my fantasies in the past six years had come close to comparing to what it was like to have her sprawled on top of me, taking her fill. Her soft curves and smooth skin were like velvet against my hardened, weather-worn body. And all I wanted to do was lose myself in her forever.

She was perfect. An angel come to life… or a naughty demon temptress. The way she was working her way down my torso, nipping and scraping her teeth over my skin, had my mind reeling. The desire for her to take my cock into her sweet mouth had me aching in anticipation.

I knew I should stop her. Shouldn't let it happen the first time. Should be careful with her and show her just how much I loved her. Make love to her with slow, gentle movements. But I was useless. Lost to the passion sparking between us.

"Hannah," I forced out, barely able to keep from flipping her over and taking her in one long, hard thrust.

She lifted her head and caught my eye just as she wrapped her small hand around my dick.

"Fuck," I said and closed my eyes, unable to watch her pleasuring me. It was too much. I'd never last.

"That's the plan." She let out a low chuckle, and in the next moment, her sweet, hot mouth was on me, tasting me. Her movements were slow, deliberate, as if she was savoring the moment.

A grunt of pleasure slipped from me as I clutched the bedcovers, willing myself to not thrust up into all her warmth.

But my appreciation seemed to spur her on because in the next moment she took me deep into her mouth until I felt myself brush the back of her throat.

"Jesus," I muttered and ground my molars together.

Her lips tightened around me, and still holding the base of my shaft, she began to move. My breathing became rapid and all I knew was her. My gorgeous Hannah was finally all mine. And I was completely hers, at her mercy to do with as she pleased.

And just when my muscles bunched and my breath started to hitch, she released me and rose up, her eyes wild. "We're not even close to being done."

She crawled back up, positioned herself over me, and reclaimed my shaft as she held it right at her opening.

I was transfixed, ensnared in her gaze, every muscle taut with pure lust.

"I want you to watch as I claim you," she

said, her voice silky and rich with desire. Casting her gaze down, she indicated our joining.

There was no denying her, not that I'd even want to. I was going to enjoy the fuck out of this. I slid my hands up her thighs, widening them even farther as she slowly lowered herself on top of me.

Her heat enveloped me, and if I hadn't had my eyes glued to her pink flesh taking me inch by inch, my eyes would've rolled into the back of my head. She was so tight and perfect as she adjusted to my intrusion with ease. I waited as she settled over me, let her lids slide closed, and sighed with deep pleasure.

"Open your eyes," I whispered.

Her lids fluttered open, brilliant green shining back at me.

"It's your turn to watch."

Her lips twitched in amusement. "What else is there to see?"

"This." I flicked my thumb over her slick clit and felt a deep satisfaction when she let out a loud gasp.

"Yes," she breathed as her eyelids started to close again.

"No, baby. I want you to watch me get you off."

Instantly, she returned her gaze to my hand as I kneaded her most sensitive spot.

"Oh my God. I can't—" Her words got caught in her throat as she started to move, grinding into me.

I met her already-frantic pace, thrusting up hard and fast, taking her deep over and over and over again, all the while keeping my thumb on her.

"More," she demanded, a feral look in her crazed eyes. She was wild, tapping into her inner wolf, needing something she couldn't name.

It was me. She needed her mate. Needed to claim me the way a wolf claimed her mate.

I gripped her hips, holding her down against me, and at my last almost violent thrust, I felt her muscles clench, just on the verge of her coming undone.

"Do it now," I coaxed, pulling her down on top of my chest. "Bite me. Make me yours."

My words were all she needed. Instinct took over, and without another word, she let out a low growl and sank her teeth into my neck.

With her bite, she exploded, her intense orgasm igniting mine. And as I gripped her ass, holding her to me, I spilled into her, coming so hard that, true to her words, I nearly did black out.

CHAPTER 9
HANNAH

It was a long time before I was able to move again. I lay on top of Silas, both impressed and mortified by my behavior. I hadn't been a virgin, but I wasn't experienced by any stretch of the imagination. And what I'd just done with Silas, how I'd talked to him… And God, the bite. Had I actually done that?

I smoothed my fingers over his already healed flesh, wondering if I'd only imagined it.

"Wolf blood," he said lazily.

Crap. Not my imagination. "Wren doesn't

heal that fast."

Which begged the question, how come I'd come out of the car crash without so much as a scratch? I knew what wolf blood could do, but usually there were minor scars or bruises for at least a few days.

"Most wolves don't. I've always been a faster-than-normal healer. Do you see any scars on this body?"

I rolled off him and took a nice long look. Not one imperfection anywhere. "I'll be damned," I said to myself.

He chuckled. "You never noticed before? I'd have bet you had every inch of me memorized."

A flush heated my face. He was right. But I'd been too busy cataloging his too-good-to-be-true muscles to notice any flaws.

He gave me a self-satisfied smile. But then he sobered as he traced his fingers just over my right eyebrow. "Like this scar you used to have here."

"Used to?" I asked. I'd earned that mark when I was eight in a bicycle accident.

"Yep. Just like this one." He moved his hand to the back of my bare thigh, indicating the fading scar I'd gotten from a rusted airboat out in the bayou. "Both are gone. Healed from the wolf blood."

My eyes widened. "You're serious?"

He nodded and pressed a light kiss just below my ear.

"Wow." I wasn't sure what to make of that. In fact, I wasn't sure what to make of any of the past few days. All I knew was that for the first time in forever, I didn't feel like I was missing something. Like I'd found a piece of my heart I hadn't even known I'd lost.

"It must be a lot to get used to," Silas said, his tone full of sympathy.

"No, it isn't." Lifting up on one elbow, I gazed down at him. "Not really. Only in the way that everything is a new experience for me. Other than that, being a wolf, your mate, it feels right. This is where I belong. With you."

His eyes brightened and a slow smile spread over his face. "That's good. Because you have to know I'm never going to let you go. Not now. Not ever."

It was my turn to smile. "What about Wren?"

"He'll get over it." Silas reached up and cupped my neck, gently pulling me down until our lips met. "But right now the last thing I want to do is talk about him. Kiss me like you mean it."

"Gladly." Our lips met, and in moments we were once again lost in each other.

I WOKE TO a commotion on the other side of our closed door. Someone was yelling and insisting we get up.

"What the hell is going on?" I said sleepily, squinting into the darkness. I had no idea what time it was, or heck, even what day it was. After we'd made love again, I'd fallen into a deep, exhausted sleep. New wolves were known to do that.

"Smoke has Thea's location. We have to go. Get up."

"Thea?" I sat up straight and had to hold my head to keep the room from spinning. "He found her?"

"Yes. And they're on the move. Get dressed or I'll have to leave you here." His tone was all business. He wasn't messing around.

"There's no way I'm staying here," I said, already pulling on the clothes someone had put beside the bed. The jeans were a size too big, but the T-shirt was the right size. I didn't care. I was just grateful there was something to wear since Skye's dress had been utterly ruined. "Give me one second." I rushed into the adjoining bathroom, freshened up, and was back in less than two minutes.

Silas grabbed my hand and together we joined Smoke and his mate Scarlett at the front door.

"It's good to see you upright," Scarlett said, handing me a takeout container.

"Thanks." I glanced at the box in my hand, my mouth already watering. The scent of cooked beef and spices filled my senses.

Scarlett eyed me. "You've got to be starving. I didn't stop eating for a week after the change."

I nodded, my stomach growling so loud I was certain the person standing across the street could hear it.

"Don't worry. There's more." She pointed to Smoke and the shopping bag he carried. "You can eat as much as you like on the way."

"How did this get here?" I asked as I climbed into the back of the resort's black SUV.

"The Jeep is a goner. I had Darien drop it off two days ago," Silas said.

I nodded, wondering what Darien and

Wren knew about my new state of being, but now wasn't the time to worry about it. Instead, I asked, "Where are we headed?"

Silas, who'd taken the driver's seat, fired up the engine and said, "They're headed toward the Northshore."

The Northshore referred to the landmass above Lake Pontchartrain, the lake that sat just north of New Orleans, separating Orleans Parish from St. Tammany Parish.

Smoke plugged his phone into the USB port and a map lit up on the console. He pressed a button and a blinking light showed up on the screen. He scowled. "Dammit. They're not wasting any time. Step on it."

Silas slammed the SUV into gear and took off.

"Who are they?" I asked between bites of

the shredded beef. "Do you know?"

Smoke glanced back at me. "Two guys with a record long enough to land them both a lifetime in prison. One of them, her "friend" Will, has ties to a well-known human trafficking ring in Russia."

Scarlett clenched her fists until her knuckles turned white, while my stomach rolled. Could this incident involve the FBI in any way? Before Scarlett mated with Smoke, she'd been with an FBI agent who was killed on the job. Only it hadn't been an accident. He'd been killed because he'd gotten too close to an inside job that had something to do with human trafficking. And to make matters worse, recently a hit man had been sent after Scarlett to eliminate her in the event that she knew anything.

Smoke and another FBI agent had gotten to

the hit man first, and even though there hadn't been another threat against Scarlett, the case hadn't been closed. Neither had the investigation into the human trafficking. The fact Will had ties to a trafficking ring was entirely too coincidental.

Everyone was silent. Then finally Smoke turned to Scarlett and in a steely tone said, "If they're involved, they'll wish they'd never been born."

CHAPTER 10
SILAS

According to the GPS, the drive to the small town of Independence should've taken us an hour and ten minutes. I got us there in forty. Hannah's friend Thea had been missing for seventy-two hours. Long enough that she could've already been sold or shipped out of the country, or worse. Now that we had a lead, I wasn't wasting another second.

It was a damned miracle we'd gotten a hit. If it hadn't been for Smoke, we wouldn't have. He was a world class hacker who worked for the FBI. But he'd done this job off the books. He didn't know who he could and couldn't trust on the inside now. Not after the attempted hit on Scarlett. We were on our own with this one unless we wanted to invite more trouble. It was a lucky break he'd been able to tap into Thea's phone and lift Will's number. With that information, he'd been off and running.

I parked the car about a half mile away from an old warehouse on a side road off State Route 40. The four of us slipped from the car silently, and with an unspoken agreement we moved toward the warehouse. At the end of a dirt driveway there was a faded sign that read *Augustine's Alligator Processing.*

Christ. There could be any number of gruesome pieces of equipment still housed in there. Just what we needed.

Hannah grabbed my arm, stopping me. "He's here."

"Who?"

"Will. I recognize his scent." Her brow was furrowed and her entire body taut with tension.

I sniffed the air, my wolf senses unable to pick up on what she had. "Are you sure?"

She nodded, her gaze fixed on the warehouse. Before I could say anything else, she took off in a sprint, her body morphing into her brindled wolf form mid-leap. The clothes she'd been wearing lay strewn behind her.

"Son of… Damn!" She was too new to control her wolf tendencies, and if she scented Will, the man who'd nearly gotten her abducted, three days before, of course her wolf would take over. My wolf rose to the surface, already following the lead of my mate. There was no stopping the shift even if I'd wanted to. My wolf wouldn't have it. I hastily pulled my clothes off, and a second later my paws had barely touched the dusty earth as I watched in horror while Hannah disappeared into the warehouse through an open window.

Shouts followed by rapid gunfire sounded from the warehouse, followed by a loud howl.

Hannah!

CHAPTER 11
HANNAH

ALL RATIONAL THOUGHT had fled with my shift. Will's scent had hit me, and the memory of him leaving me with my attacker hit me hard. There was no stopping the shift. No way to hold myself back from going after my prey.

I was on autopilot, a wolf with a mission. To take down the predator who liked to hurt women. In my wolf form, my agile body flew effortlessly through the open window and I landed with a snarl on a cement floor, my jaws bared and my hackles raised.

"Holy fuck!" A tall man wearing blue coveralls cried out and jumped back behind a crate.

The other one, the one I recognized as Will, recovered from the shock of seeing me much faster and calmly pulled out his gun. Without ceremony, he opened fire.

I let out a loud howl and scrambled, taking cover behind a large wooden worktable.

"What the fuck was that?" Skinny cried.

"One of those shifters," Will shot back, the sound of his voice carrying through the room as if he was moving closer to me.

He knew about us? Since when? I glanced around and caught a glimpse of a metal cage. Flattening myself to the floor, I peeked around the wooden table and spotted Thea. She was curled in a ball, hugging her knees while she rocked in the corner of her cell. Naked. My eyes narrowed, and a primal urge to kill the son of a bitch took over.

"Did Shade send them?" Skinny asked.

"Why the fuck would he do that?"

"I don't know. He's the only shifter I've ever met."

The word *shifter* penetrated my revenge haze, escalating the rage that was already eating me from the inside out. I crept forward, keeping my head down, and spotted the grimy shoes of my victim. Just two more steps and—

There was a commotion, and the sound of breaking glass came from near the window I'd crashed through, followed by Silas's growl and the shouts of Smoke and Scarlett as they demanded Will and his partner stand down.

Will stopped in his tracks and brandished

his gun once more.

No!

I leaped, my jaws clamping around his wrist. The gun went off, followed by more gunfire. My heart got lodged in my throat, but it was too late to stop. If I let go before Will dropped his gun, I'd be his next victim.

Never again.

The words rolled through my head as I growled and clamped down harder on his arm.

He screamed and thrashed as I knocked him down, using my weight to keep him pinned to the floor. But he still had a free arm, and before I could scramble out of the way, he swung, catching me in the head.

My world spun, but I didn't let go, my fight instinct fully intact. Again and again, he swung, knocking his fist against my head, relentlessly trying to free himself. But after the third blow, I dropped his bloody arm and lunged, going for his throat. I missed and caught his shirt, tearing it down the middle, exposing another gun tucked into his waistband. He reached for it with his good hand, but this time I was too fast. I caught his neck in my jaws and felt a gush of blood fill my mouth.

He gurgled and before I knew it, his body stilled beneath me.

"Hannah?" Scarlett asked, her tone soft as she stood next to me.

I growled.

"It's all right, hon. You can let go now. He's no longer a threat."

I cut my gaze to the cage where I'd seen Thea earlier, only to find the door open and the cage empty. That was enough. I let go and backed off, keeping my shoulders hunched just in case I needed to attack again.

"It's all right. Silas?" she called.

I followed her gaze and spotted my mate limping toward me. I stood up tall and trotted over to him, scenting the copper tang of blood seeping from his hind leg. When he neared me, I whined.

He pressed his head against mine, instantly soothing my nerves. We were here, together. Relatively safe.

"Well," someone I didn't know said. "Looks like you've done my job for me again."

Silas and I both spun and spotted a man in khaki slacks and a blue button-down shirt.

"Shade," Smoke said. "It's interesting how you keep showing up after we take down the bad guys."

He sent Smoke a smug smile. "Only because you keep leading me to them." He waved toward me and Silas. "Do those two belong to you?"

Smoke nodded. "Even though their tactics leave a lot to be desired, they're the ones who just took down your perps. You probably owe them a thank-you."

The agent turned to us and gave us a nod of acknowledgment. "Thanks. I appreciate the help. But you might want to shift now. The forensic crew is on their way."

"Shit," Smoke said. "Silas? That's our cue."

My mate cast me a side-eye glance and then shifted right there in front of everyone. Completely naked and with his head held high, he stood up straight. "Thanks for the warning." He glanced at me. "It's time Hannah. We need to go."

No way was I shifting in front of all of them. Earlier I hadn't been able to control it. But now? I wasn't even sure if I knew how.

"Let's go, Hannah," Scarlett said. "You can shift in the car."

I cast her what I hoped was a thankful glance and then followed her out of the warehouse.

Once we made it back to the car, I jumped in and lay in the back seat, willing myself to return to my human form. Nothing happened. I closed my eyes and tried again. A faint tingle sparked through my limbs but fizzled out before anything happened.

"She needs Silas," I heard Scarlett say.

"He's still in the warehouse," Smoke said.

The mention of Silas's name was enough.

The spark grew and there was a tug deep in my belly followed by the lengthening of my limbs as I completed my shift. When I was back in human form, I sat straight up, shivering in the cool spring air. "Uh, Scarlett?"

"Hannah?" She poked her head into the SUV, her eyes wide with surprise. "Well, look at you. Welcome back."

"Are there any clothes around here?"

She chuckled. "You mean these? They're a little dusty, but they should do." She tossed me the clothes I'd borrowed earlier in the day.

"Thanks." I hastily pulled the clothes on, grateful I hadn't damaged them in my shift, and then took off barefoot back to the warehouse. I needed to know Will's fate. The thought of him made my throat close. Had I killed him?

A feeling of doom settled in my chest. As a

wolf, I hadn't cared. As a human, the thought made me sick to my stomach. I sped up, jogging the rest of the way.

"What's going to happen to him?" Silas asked Shade.

A memory came roaring back. Hadn't the skinny guy said something about knowing him? I frowned, watching the exchange between my mate and the FBI agent.

"He'll stand trial for abduction and we'll do our best to get information from him on the trafficking ring."

"You're sure he's a part of it?" Silas glanced over at the cage, and I was vindicated to see the bastard was propped up in the cell, his eyes fixated on Shade. He was alive. Thank God. Killing someone, even a scumbag like him, wasn't on my agenda my first night out as a shifter.

"Yes," Thea said, her voice coming from behind me. "I heard him talking about the drop point."

I spun, finding my friend wrapped in a thin gray blanket. "Thea!"

Tears welled in her big brown eyes. "I'm so sorry. I can't believe I tried to set you up with that monster."

I stood there, shock rendering me speechless. Then I moved and caught her in a bear hug. "You have nothing to be sorry for. He's the one who's a sick bastard. If we hadn't..." My voice was thick with emotion. "Thank God we got here in time."

She returned my embrace, and after a moment, she shook as she silently wept into my shoulder.

Silas joined us and in a very quiet voice he said, "I don't want to rush you, but if we're here when forensics gets here, it's going to be ugly. Shade said he'll come up with a cover for what went down."

"What about Thea?" I asked, still rubbing her back.

"She's coming with us." Silas put an arm around each of us and steered us out of the old, dusty warehouse.

When we got back to the SUV, Smoke was punching something into his phone, frowning.

"What is it?" Silas asked.

He glanced up, confusion lining his face. "I can't figure it out."

"What?"

"How he tracked me." He jerked his head toward the warehouse. "This phone is fairly new, and I can't find any traces of trackers or programs anywhere."

Scarlett put her hand on his shoulder. "He is the only one who's managed to break into your home system."

"Only because I left an opening." Smoke's eyes narrowed in concentration. "I just don't see how it was possible. Unless he was tracking the SUV." He turned his attention to the truck.

"It's possible," I said. "You did put the GPS through the dash console."

He nodded. "I guess you're right. I'll have to strip it down when we get back."

"Fine," Silas said. "But right now we have to go." He held the back door open for me, Scarlett, and Thea. Scarlett climbed into the back, leaving the middle seat for me and Thea, while the guys once again sat up front.

"Where are we going?" Thea asked, her voice still thick with tears.

I met Silas's eyes in the rearview mirror and said, "Home."

CHAPTER 12
SILAS

Home was my cabin at the resort. We'd rescued Thea a week ago. Since then the three of us hadn't left the resort once. Thea was too scared. Hannah and I were too content.

Thea's ordeal had been more than she could handle, but after spending a week curled up in Hannah's old cabin, she was starting to show signs of life. As for Hannah, she'd moved into my place without hesitation the night we'd gotten back.

Wren was pissed as hell, but there wasn't

anything he could do about it. We were already mated. Darien was mostly staying out of it and spent the majority of his time keeping Thea company. Which was for the best. She needed someone neutral, someone she trusted, to talk to.

Hannah and I were relaxing on my front porch when Smoke rolled up in my SUV. He'd taken it the night we'd gotten back, determined to find whatever bug Shade had used to follow us.

He hopped out and took the steps two at a time onto my porch. "Well. It's clean."

I raised my eyebrows. "You're sure?"

He nodded. "I had a buddy of mine who's somewhat of an expert sweep it. It's clean."

"And still no sign of a trace on your phone?"

"No sign." He pressed his lips together in a thin line. "I gotta tell you, there's something off about all this. That's twice now that Shade's shown up right after we've taken down the bad guys."

"I thought he was Bax's partner. Fischer is his last name, right?" Hannah asked. "Isn't he the one that warned Scarlett about the threat against her life?"

"Yeah. That's why I can't wrap my head around this. If he was behind Scarlett's attack, why would he warn her? On the other hand, I can't figure out how he found us at that warehouse. Or why he cared so much about us getting out of there. Something's not adding up."

I glanced over at Hannah's old cabin. "Maybe Thea has some answers."

Hannah shook her head. "I don't think so. She says all they told her was that as soon as their Russian friend arrived, they'd be rid of her and flush again. Apparently they were going to sell her off."

Smoke closed his eyes and shook his head. "Pieces of shit."

I couldn't agree more. "You think we need to investigate Shade?"

"Maybe. Like I said, something's not right there."

A white Ford truck pulled up behind my SUV, and Scarlett poked her head out, waving to us.

"That's my ride. Scarlett's not sure my hunch is correct. She's known him a long time, but if we don't look into this and it turns out to be something… I can't live with that."

"I'm behind you, brother," I said and clasped his hand. "Whatever you need, I'll be here."

"Thanks. I'll start digging around and let you know what I find."

"Be careful." Smoke was on probation for an illegal hacking charge six years ago. As part of his condition for release, he had to work for the FBI. If he was caught breaking any laws, he'd wind up right back in jail to serve his entire sentence.

"Will do." He gave Silas a mock salute and hightailed it to the truck.

I reached over and grabbed Hannah's hand as we watched them drive off. "You okay?"

"Yeah. You?"

I turned and smiled at her. "I will be, just as soon as I get you back into our bed."

"Our bed?" Her lips quirked up as she raised her eyebrows, her expression questioning.

"Well, yeah. You didn't think you were moving back into your cabin once Thea leaves, did you?"

She shook her head. "No, wouldn't dream of it. But I was thinking we could maybe add a few feminine touches. You know, maybe a new bedspread, softer sheets, and a fuzzy blanket."

"Whatever you want, babe. Just as long as you're there. Naked."

She laughed. "Where else would I be?"

"You heard the naked part, right?" I asked as I nuzzled her neck.

"Sure. In fact I was just thinking I was feeling a little overdressed." She slid her small hand down, letting her fingers linger at my belt buckle.

I let out a low growl, tracing my fingers over her jawline. "Don't start things you don't intend to finish."

"Who says I don't intend to finish?" There was a glint of challenge in her eyes.

"Aren't you supposed to be working right now?"

She shrugged. "Yes. But I don't think I'm going to get fired or anything. You see, I know the owner."

"Is that right?" I stared at her full lips as she darted her tongue out. "And you think he's willing to overlook you shirking your duties."

"He will if I make him come hard enough."

Christ. Her words made me instantly hard. I stood, lifting her into my arms as I rose. Her legs wrapped around me, and I carried her inside, straight into our bedroom. "Let's see what you've got, Valentine."

She laughed, slid down my body, and reached once again for the button of my jeans. "You first, Davenne."

"Gladly." Less than a minute later, we were naked and I was settling between her legs, my tip already pressing into her.

"Is this what you had in mind?" I asked.

"More like this." She grabbed my ass and yanked me down, forcing me to thrust into her.

She let out a low, self-satisfied moan while I reveled in her boldness. Jesus. All that time I'd thought she was too innocent for me. Too sweet. I'd been dead wrong. Hannah was my match in every way. Strong, passionate, and so fucking perfect.

"I'm ready for you to make me come," I

whispered into her ear.

"I bet you are." Then she grinned as she tightened herself around me. "But I think I'll make you work for it. I believe you still have two more fantasies to show me."

"Greedy."

She grinned up at me, triumph glittering in her gaze. "True. And you wouldn't have it any other way."

Sign up for Kenzie's newsletter at www.kenziecox.com to be notified of new releases. Do you prefer text messages? Sign up for text alerts! Just text SHIFTERSROCK to 24587 to register.

Book List:

Wolves of the Rising Sun

Jace

Aiden

Luc

Craved

Silas

Darien

Wren

Printed in Great Britain
by Amazon